Jeffrey's Ghost and the Leftover Baseball Team

DAVID A. ADLER

◆

JEFFREY'S GHOST

and the Leftover Baseball Team

◆

Illustrated by
JEAN JENKINS

Holt, Rinehart and Winston ◆ New York

To Alice Spechler

Published by Holt, Rinehart and Winston,
383 Madison Avenue, New York, New York 10017.

Published simultaneously in Canada by Holt, Rinehart
and Winston of Canada, Limited.

Library of Congress Cataloging in Publication Data
Adler, David A.
Jeffrey's ghost and the leftover baseball team.

Summary: A baseball team of children no one else
wants on a team turns into a team of winners with the
help of a friendly boy ghost.
[1. Baseball—Fiction.   2. Ghosts—Fiction]
I. Jenkins, Jean, ill.   II. Title.
PZ7.A2615Je   1984   [Fic]   83-22662
ISBN: 0-03-069282-2

Designer: Victoria Hartman
Printed in the United States of America
5 7 9 10 8 6 4

ISBN 0-03-069282-2

Jeffrey's Ghost and the Leftover Baseball Team

Chapter

·1·

A book floated out of a carton and into the bookshelf. Pencils floated out of another carton. The top desk drawer opened by itself and the pencils floated in.

"This place is weird," Jeffrey Clark said. He sat on his bed and watched as his books, shoes, and shirts floated to where they belonged.

Jeffrey was ten years old. He was thin and had curly brown hair. He and his parents had just moved. Before they moved, Jeffrey had slept in the living room. Now their apartment was the whole second floor of an old house and Jeffrey had his own room. He was just beginning to put his things away when they began to float into place by themselves.

Another box opened. A huge pair of red pants floated up and headed toward the closet.

"Hey, those aren't mine," Jeffrey said. "Those are Dad's golf pants."

"I'm only trying to help," a loud, deep voice answered. It seemed to come from the red pants.

"I know you're trying to help," Jeffrey's mother called from her room. "And I appreciate it."

"All right," Jeffrey whispered, "who said that?"

"I think it was your mother," the voice whispered back.

"I know who *she* is, but who are *you*? And what are you?"

"I'm Bradford. I've lived here since this house was built. People could see me until I was ten. Then while I was cleaning the barn a horse kicked me. That's when I became invisible."

"Then you're a . . . a . . . ghost!"

"Well," Bradford said, "some people call me that."

Jeffrey just sat there on his bed. He didn't know what to do. He knew that he should be frightened of a ghost, but Bradford just didn't seem frightening.

Jeffrey's bed creaked. A large crease formed in the blanket. Bradford had sat down next to Jeffrey.

Jeffrey sat there quietly for a while. Then he felt Bradford pat him on the back.

"Come on," Bradford said. "Let's finish un-packing."

Chapter

·2·

Bradford and Jeffrey worked together. Bradford unpacked the boxes while Jeffrey put everything away. When they finished, Bradford said, "I'm going to the park to join a baseball team. Do you want to come along?"

"Sure."

Jeffrey put on his sneakers. He took his baseball glove and went to his parents' room. Jeffrey's father was up on a ladder hanging curtains. His mother was hanging a picture.

While Jeffrey was asking his parents if he could go outside, he saw a dress float into the air. Jeffrey ran to it before his parents could see what was happening. His mother turned and saw him holding the dress.

"You don't have to help," she said. "Go ahead to the park."

Once they were outside Jeffrey asked, "But how can a ghost be on a baseball team?"

"I tried out for some of the other teams,"

Bradford said. "No one could see me, so I didn't get to play. But this team is for leftovers. It's for the kids the other teams didn't want, so I should be able to play on it."

"I didn't live here when the other teams were being formed," Jeffrey said. "But if this team is for leftovers, I guess I can join too."

When Jeffrey and Bradford reached the park, an old man was standing at home plate. He was hitting a baseball to some children in the field.

"Go on," the man called to Jeffrey. "Take second base."

Jeffrey ran onto the field.

Crack!

The ball was hit along the ground. It flew across the grass toward the space between Jeffrey and the girl playing shortstop. The girl ran toward the ball. So did Jeffrey. But it was out of their reach.

Then it happened. Just as the ball was about to go past them, it stopped. It bounced up, hung in the air for a moment, and then flew to the first baseman.

"Who caught that?" the man at home plate called out.

"I did," Bradford answered. But of course no one could see him.

"Nice play," the man, the girl playing shortstop, and a few of the other children called to Jeffrey.

The old man continued to hit the baseball into the field. Laura, the girl playing shortstop, and Jeffrey caught it a few times. So did Bradford.

Each time Bradford caught the ball, Jeffrey ran to it. Jeffrey made it look like he had fielded the ball. He didn't want the others to know that there was a ghost nearby. Jeffrey thought it might frighten them.

Then the old man called, "Everyone come here, please. I want to talk to you."

As they were running off the field, Laura said to Jeffrey, "You really made some great catches. It almost seemed like the ball stopped and waited for you to pick it up."

Jeffrey sat on a bench near the old man.

"Tell her *I* caught the ball," Bradford whispered to Jeffrey.

"Sh."

"Go on, tell her."

"My name is Jackson Evers," the old man said.

"I'm glad all of you came to try out for the team. We'll be playing in the Summer League. It's for children between the ages of eight and twelve."

"I caught the ball," Bradford whispered to Laura.

"Quiet!" Laura said to Jeffrey. "I'm trying to listen to Mr. Evers."

"For the past few years," Mr. Evers went on, "I helped coach the Zebras. They were last year's champions. But this year they didn't want me. They said I was too old."

One boy said, "They told me to come back when I learn how to play."

"I tried out for the Lions," Laura told Jeffrey. "But they didn't want a girl on their team."

"That's terrible," Bradford whispered.

Mr. Evers said, "I was upset when they told me I couldn't coach. Then I thought about all the children who have been told they couldn't play on a team. That's when I decided to start a team of my own, a team for leftovers."

Mr. Evers handed some forms to the boy sitting closest to him. "Your parents will have to sign these. And this is our schedule," he said as he handed the same boy some more papers.

"What's the name of our team?" someone asked.

"That's up to you," Mr. Evers said.

"Let's call ourselves the Green Socks," a boy wearing green socks called out.

"How about the Sluggers?"

"Tigers."

The papers were passed to Jeffrey. He took one of each and handed them to Laura.

The papers flew out of Laura's hands. She pulled them back.

"What about me?" Bradford asked. "I need a schedule too."

"Who said that?" asked Laura.

"I did."

"Who are you? Why can't I see you?"

"That's Bradford," Jeffrey whispered. "He's invisible."

"What do you mean, 'He's invisible'?"

"I mean you can't see him."

"Then he's a . . ." Laura dropped the papers she was holding. "Then he's a . . ." Laura stood up, stretched out her arms in horror, and yelled, "Then he's a ghost!"

Chapter

·3·

The other children on the team turned and looked at Laura. Mr. Evers looked too. "You didn't have to shout," Mr. Evers said, "but thank you. That's a great name for the team. Let's call ourselves the Ghosts."

Mr. Evers clapped his hands and said, "All right, Ghosts, I'll see you all here tomorrow for practice."

Laura and Jeffrey just sat there as the other children walked off the field. Then Mr. Evers went to his car and drove off.

"A horse kicked him," Jeffrey told Laura once everyone else had gone. "That's when he became invisible."

There was an old torn baseball on the field. It floated up.

"Let's play catch," Bradford said. Then the ball flew into Laura's hands.

"Don't be afraid of Bradford," Jeffrey said. "He's really very nice."

Laura threw the ball to Jeffrey. He threw it back to Laura.

"What about me?" Bradford asked.

Laura threw the ball to where she thought Bradford was standing. The ball stopped in midair. Then it flew to Jeffrey.

Jeffrey, Laura, and Bradford played for several minutes. Then they heard voices.

"There must be a big glass wall over there. He throws the ball against the wall and it bounces back."

"No, it's a boomerang ball."

Jeffrey and Laura turned around. A few people were standing behind the fence.

"A boomerang is a special kind of bent stick," one boy said. "There's no such thing as a boomerang ball."

"Well, then," a woman carrying a leather briefcase said, "maybe the ball is tied to a long elastic band."

"How do you do it?" a man asked Jeffrey.

"We're not doing anything special," Jeffrey told them.

"We're just playing catch with Bradford," Laura said. "You just can't see Bradford because he's a ghost."

"That's nonsense," one of the men said.

"Is there really a ghost?" a small girl asked the woman with the briefcase.

"Of course not," the woman said. "There's no such thing as a ghost."

As soon as she said it, the woman's briefcase opened. A folder flew out and landed on the ground. When the woman bent to pick it up, it moved. It kept moving and the woman chased after it. The folder went under and

13

around trees and onto the baseball field. Then it flew into a large trash basket. The woman covered the basket with her brief-case. When she was sure the folder had stopped moving, she took it out. She put the folder in her briefcase and walked off.

While the woman was chasing after the folder, Laura was laughing.

"You shouldn't have done that," Jeffrey told Bradford after everyone had gone.

"Well," Bradford said, "she shouldn't have said that there are no ghosts."

"I think it was funny," Laura said. "And Bradford is right. She shouldn't have said that. If she had said there are no boys, I'll bet that you would have been angry."

Laura picked up her glove and the two pa-pers Mr. Evers had handed out.

"I'll see you two tomorrow morning at practice," she said. Then she laughed and added, "No, I guess I'll just see one of you."

Chapter

·4·

Bradford picked up the ball. He threw it up and caught it as he walked out of the park. To Jeffrey it looked like the ball was bouncing in midair without touching the ground.

"Come on," Bradford called to Jeffrey. "Let's go home."

"Do you mean you plan to live with us?" Jeffrey asked.

"No," Bradford said, "I think you plan to live with me. When that horse kicked me, I was living on a farm, and the house you moved into today is right where our barn once stood. I've been living in the same place for over two hundred years."

As they walked, Bradford pointed out where Grover Cleveland, the President, once sat and watched a parade. He showed Jeffrey some old trolly-car tracks and the tree a college boy once sat in for over one hundred hours. The college boy did it to win a bet.

Before they went into the house, Jeffrey whispered to Bradford, "Let's not let my parents know that you're here. They might not understand."

"Is that you?" Jeffrey's mother called as he opened the door.

"Yes."

"Come to the kitchen. We're eating lunch."

When Jeffrey sat down, his mother gave him a big serving of cheese and noodles. "I expect you to eat it all," she said.

Jeffrey poked his fork into a pile of noodles. He pulled one out and ate it slowly. While Jeffrey ate, so did Bradford. The noodles were quickly gone.

The dessert was Jeffrey's favorite, nut layer cake. Jeffrey cut his slice in half. He ate one piece and left the second half for Bradford.

"You can have it," Bradford said. "I don't like nut cake."

Jeffrey's mother heard Bradford. "But I thought nut cake was your favorite," she said.

"It is, Mom, it is," Jeffrey told her and quickly finished the cake.

16

Jeffrey worked all afternoon unpacking his books and games. Bradford helped. At night Jeffrey slept in his bed. Bradford slept in a chair with his feet up on the desk.

When Jeffrey and Bradford came to the park the next morning, a group of children was already crowded around home plate. Jackson Evers was in the middle of the group dividing them into two teams.

"Is he here?" Laura whispered to Jeffrey.

"Bradford came with me," Jeffrey whispered, "but I don't know where he is."

Jackson Evers pointed to Jeffrey. "What's your name?" he asked.

"Jeffrey Clark."

"All right, Jeffrey, you'll play second base for the B team. Laura, you'll play shortstop."

The B team was in the field first. Jeffrey and Laura stood at their positions and waited. The first ball was hit along the ground. The third baseman ran to his right and caught it. He had made a good play, but he made a poor throw to first base. The runner was safe.

For the first few innings that's how the game went. There were some good plays in the field and there were errors. Two balls were hit to Jeffrey. He caught the first one, but in the third inning he dropped an easy fly ball.

As they were walking back to the bench Laura asked Jeffrey, "What happened? You were much better yesterday."

"No, I wasn't. Bradford was helping me. Now I don't know where he is."

Jeffrey picked up a bat. He was up next. He took a practice swing.

"Ouch!"

"What?"

"I said ouch. You hit me in the stomach." It was Bradford. "You should be more careful."

Jeffrey stood in the batter's box. The pitcher was getting ready to throw the ball. Jeffrey held his bat up. Something pulled it down.

"Don't hold your bat so high," Bradford whispered.

Jeffrey held his bat up again and Bradford pulled it lower. Just then the ball was thrown.

"Strike one," Mr. Evers called.

"Listen to me," Bradford whispered

Jeffrey turned and said, "Leave me alone," just as the next pitch was thrown.

"Strike two."

Jeffrey tried to swing at the next pitch, but Bradford held his bat. "You're not swinging level," he whispered.

"Strike three. You're out."

Jeffrey dropped his bat and walked back to the bench. "It was Bradford," he told Laura. "He kept getting in the way."

"I was helping," Bradford whispered. "And believe me, this team needs help. Too many of you don't know how to hold a bat. Most of you need help catching the ball too."

Bradford sat on the bench between Jeffrey and Laura. He pulled them close and whispered, "I can help this team. I know just what to do."

Chapter

·5·

"What? What are you going to do?" Jeffrey asked. But Bradford didn't answer. He was gone.

Jeffrey picked his baseball glove up off the ground. He put it on and punched his fist into the pocket a few times.

"Wow! Did you see that?" Laura asked as she clapped her hands.

"What happened?"

"A line drive was hit right over third base. Paul dove for it."

"So what. Paul is always jumping and diving for balls. But he never catches any."

"This time he did. He caught it in the webbing of his glove. You should have seen Paul's face when he caught it. He was real surprised."

The next batter hit a fly ball into the outfield. Michael, the left fielder, ran for it. The ball seemed out of his reach. But he caught it for the third out.

"It's Bradford," Jeffrey told Laura as they walked back onto the field. "I think he helped Paul and Michael catch those last two balls."

During the next few innings there were a few more good plays. And there were no er-

rors. One ball that was hit toward Jeffrey seemed to stop and wait for him to pick it up. Just as he was about to throw it to first base Bradford whispered, "Don't rush. Throw it nice and easy."

After the game Jackson Evers called the players of both teams together. First he collected the forms their parents had signed. Then he told them, "At first your fielding was sloppy. I was worried. But after the third inning you played like champions."

A few of the kids clapped and cheered.

"Tomorrow morning is our first game. We play the Lions. The game starts at ten o'clock. Just play like you did today and we can beat them. I know we can."

Everyone cheered.

Mr. Evers smiled. He picked up his papers and started to walk toward his car when Laura asked, "What about uniforms?"

"Oh, yes," Jackson Evers said. "We don't have the time to have real uniforms made. We don't have the money either. So I want each of you to write 'Ghosts' on the front of a white T-shirt. On the back write the number I give you."

Jackson Evers called the names of each player. He gave them each a number. Jeffrey's number was six. Laura's was twelve.

"Did you see that?" Bradford asked as he walked home with Jeffrey. "Did you see Paul's face when he caught that ball? And that high pop-up. The boy at first base closed his eyes and held up his glove. I pushed the ball into his glove. He just couldn't believe he caught it."

Bradford and Jeffrey were standing at a corner, waiting for the traffic light to turn green.

"Will you help us during tomorrow's game?" Jeffrey asked.

"What's that?"

Jeffrey spoke louder. "I said, 'Will you help us during tomorrow's game?'"

"I still can't hear you," someone behind Jeffrey said.

Jeffrey turned around. An old woman was standing there. She held the handle of a small shopping cart with one hand. With the other she tapped her hearing aid. "It's the batteries," she said in a loud voice. "I think I need new batteries."

Jeffrey nodded. When the light turned green he helped the woman across the street.

Jeffrey walked home alone, or at least he thought he was alone. When he reached the tree that the college boy once sat in, Bradford said, "No, I can't help you tomorrow. If I did, it wouldn't be fair to the other team."

"I'm not talking to you," Jeffrey mumbled. "No one can see you. People walking by must think I'm talking to myself. They must think I'm crazy."

A man walking toward Jeffrey heard him mumbling. He smiled as he walked by.

"It was fun helping you today," Bradford whispered as they walked. "I ran all over the field catching balls and pushing them into kids' gloves."

"What good will that do us tomorrow when we play the Lions?"

"Listen to me," Bradford said. "I've seen all the great ones play—Hank Aaron, Babe Ruth, Ted Williams, and Ty Cobb. And I saw Pete Timbers play too."

"Who is Pete Timbers?"

"Pete could have been a great player. He

would run for a ball, but always at the last moment he gave up. He didn't think he could catch the ball. Pete could have been a great player if only he had a little confidence in himself. But he didn't, and today no one knows who he is. Today I gave your team some confidence. Your friends went home today thinking they can win. Well, maybe they can."

Chapter

·6·

The park was crowded the next morning. Parents, brothers, and sisters of some of the players had come to watch the game. Babies were crying. Little children ran onto the field. Their parents went after them. Some of the players on Jeffrey's team stood together in small groups and talked. Others stood alone and waited for the game to start. This was the team's first game and the players were nervous.

Jackson Evers gathered his team. "Jimmy Kessler," he said, "you'll play right field and bat first."

"Did you see Paul's shirt?" Bradford whispered to Jeffrey.

"Sh."

"Laura Robbins, you'll play shortstop and bat second."

"Look at Paul," Bradford said, a little louder this time.

"Sh, I'm trying to listen to the coach."

"Look at Paul's shirt!" Bradford said. This time he spoke loud enough for the whole team to hear.

Everyone turned and looked at Paul. He looked down at his shirt. He had written the team's name on the front of his shirt, but he spelled it "Goats" instead of "Ghosts."

"Do I look like a goat or do I look like a ghost?" Bradford asked.

"Sh," Jeffrey and Laura said.

"I'm no goat. I don't have horns. I don't eat paste and junk."

"Sh."

Mr. Evers wiped his eyeglasses and put them back on. "I don't know which of you is talking, but it's nothing to be so upset about."

Mr. Evers continued to read his lineup card. Jeffrey was batting seventh and playing second base.

"The coach is right," Laura whispered to Bradford. "Paul is the goat, not you."

The game started. The Ghosts were in the field first. Jeffrey stood near second base and waited.

Bradford tapped him on the shoulder. "I hope you don't mind if I stay here with you. It's lonely sitting by myself on the bench."

"Just don't get in my way."

The Ghosts' pitcher looked across the field. His players were ready. He looked in at his catcher. The batter held his bat back and waited.

"Hit it to the shortstop," one of the players on the Lions called out. "She can't catch."

While Jeffrey watched the batter, he told Bradford, "This is the team that didn't want Laura. They didn't want a girl on their team."

The batter swung at and missed the first pitch.

"They'll be sorry," Bradford said.

The next ball was hit on the ground to third base. It rolled under Paul's glove and then took a strange bounce right to Laura. She quickly threw the ball to first base. The batter was out.

"Lucky play," one of the Lions' players said as he walked toward home plate. He was the next batter.

"That's Billy Lawson," Laura told Jeffrey.

"I'm hitting this one right to you, girlie," Billy said. He stood with his feet close together and his bat held back. While Billy waited for the first pitch, something was happening to his shoelaces. But Billy didn't feel it.

Billy swung at the first pitch and hit it to Laura. As she fielded it she heard Jeffrey and some of the other Ghosts laughing. Then she saw why. Billy Lawson's shoelaces were tied together. He kept falling as he tried to run. Laura took her time and threw the ball to first base. Billy was out.

The next batter hit a fly ball. The center fielder caught it and it was the Ghosts' turn to bat.

As Jeffrey walked toward the bench, Bradford whispered in his ear, "How am I doing?"

"But I thought you weren't going to help us."

"I'm only helping Laura. The Lions will be sorry they didn't want her on their team."

Laura sat on the bench next to Jeffrey. "This game is really weird," she whispered to Jeffrey. "With Bradford out there, who knows what will be happening next."

Laura was right. It *was* a weird game.

Billy Lawson was playing shortstop for the Lions. While he stood in the field waiting for the ball to be hit he shouted, "Come on, these Ghosts can't play. Everyone knows there's no such thing as a ghost."

As soon as Billy said, "There's no such thing as a ghost," he started to laugh. The glove dropped off his hand. He started rolling

HAW HEE HEE HAW

on the ground, laughing and saying, "Stop it. Stop tickling me. Stop it."

Jackson Evers and the Lions' coach ran to Billy. Billy's teammates gathered around him. Billy had stopped laughing. He stood up, tucked his shirt back into his pants. "My undershirt must be too tight. That's what made me laugh," he said as he walked around. Then he said he was ready to play.

When Laura batted for the first time, she hit a slow ground ball right back to the Lions' pitcher. But when he bent down to pick it up, the ball moved backward. While Laura ran to first, the ball kept rolling in a crazy pattern all over the infield. By the time the pitcher got hold of the ball, Laura was standing safely on second base.

Every time Billy Lawson tried to catch a ball, his glove fell off. Every time he tried to swing a bat, it fell out of his hands.

The Ghosts won the game 7 to 3. After the last out, a few of the Ghosts' players threw their hats and gloves into the air and cheered. They all ran to the pitcher, shook his hand, and patted him on the back.

Mr. Evers said it was the strangest game he had ever seen. But he was glad that his team had won. After the game the Lions' coach told Laura that she had played well. "Maybe next year," he said, "you'll play for our team."

Jeffrey, Bradford, and Laura left the park together. They talked and laughed about the game. Bradford said that the Ghosts had played well. They would have won even without his help.

"We don't have a game tomorrow," Laura said to Jeffrey when they stood in front of her house. "Since you just moved here, why don't I show you the school, the library, and the rest of the town?"

"And I'll show both of you where I saw a car for the first time," Bradford said. "It was raining and the car got stuck in the mud. People yelled at the driver, 'Get a horse! Get a horse!'"

Jeffrey laughed and said, "You can both show me the town."

Chapter

·7·

The next morning Jeffrey and Bradford walked to Laura's house. She was outside watching her younger brother ride a tricycle.

"This is Gary," Laura said. "And this is Jeffrey."

One of Gary's toys, a plastic duck, floated up from the ground. "Tell Gary that you're going to do some magic," Bradford whispered to Jeffrey.

"I'm going to do some magic," Jeffrey said.

The duck floated over Jeffrey's head. Jeffrey held out his hands and the duck floated above them.

"I'm juggling," Jeffrey said.

Gary watched as the plastic duck climbed a tree, rode the tricycle, and opened the front door of Laura's house and went inside.

Gary and Laura followed the duck into the

house. Gary told his mother about Laura's new friend who could make toy ducks fly. And Laura told her that she was going for a walk with Jeffrey.

Laura, Jeffrey, and Bradford walked past the railroad station. A few men and women were waiting for the train to take them to the city. At the library Jeffrey signed a form and was given a library card. He took out two books, *How to Play Second Base* and *All About Ghosts*.

Outside the library Bradford pointed to the corner where he saw his first car. "People made fun of it, but soon the streets were jammed with cars."

Laura showed Jeffrey the school. It had a large playground crowded with children and their parents. Bradford played on the swings while Laura and Jeffrey looked through the windows of Laura's old classroom. In September, when the school year would begin, Laura and Jeffrey would be in the fifth grade.

During the next few weeks, Jeffrey met Laura's friends. Laura watched as Jeffrey and Bradford practiced magic together. With

Bradford's help, Jeffrey could make coins disappear and shuffle a deck of cards without touching them.

Jeffrey and Laura also played baseball.

The Ghosts were playing well, even without Bradford's help. During the games, Bradford either sat on the team bench and watched or stayed in the stands with the other fans. During one game Jeffrey hit a single with the bases loaded. Bradford got so excited that he jumped up and cheered for Jeffrey and the Ghosts. The fans sitting near Bradford turned and looked at each other. They heard Bradford cheering, but they didn't see him. Bradford quickly sat down.

Bradford came onto the field only a few times during the games. When one little boy cried because he was having trouble hitting the ball, Bradford helped him. The boy hit a double. Another boy said he thought that Ghosts was a funny name for a baseball team. Bradford opened the boy's belt and his pants fell. And when one boy dropped an easy fly ball, a woman in the stands called him butterfingers. Bradford made the soda the woman was holding fall from her hands. Then he whispered in her ear, "You're a butterfingers too."

After the ninth game Jackson Evers called his team together. "The day after tomorrow we'll play our last game," he said. "I want you to know that even if we lose that game, even if we'd lost all our games, I would still be proud to be your coach."

After the others had gone, Laura and Jef-

frey sat on the bench and talked for a while.

"Our last game is against the Zebras," Laura said. "They're the team that told Mr. Evers he was too old to coach."

"What's their record?"

"Six wins, three losses. The same as ours. We're tied for first place."

Bradford had found an old baseball. He threw it to Jeffrey. Then Jeffrey, Laura, and Bradford played catch just like they did the first day they met.

Bradford stood on second base. He didn't move from there, so Jeffrey and Laura knew where to throw the ball. They played until they heard a loud noise. It sounded like thunder.

"Let's stop," Jeffrey said. "I think it's going to rain."

"No, it's not," Bradford said. "I just sneezed." He sneezed again.

"You sneeze loud," Laura said.

"It used to scare the cows and horses," Bradford said. "Whenever I sneezed, they ran into the barn."

As they walked home, Laura said,

"Wouldn't it be great if we could beat the Zebras. Then we would be the champions."

"Bradford, do you think you could help us?" Jeffrey asked.

But Bradford didn't answer.

Chapter

·8·

As Jeffrey and Laura walked home they tried to find out if Bradford was walking with them. First they talked to him, but Bradford didn't answer. Then they teased him. They even said, "There's no such thing as a ghost." But nothing happened.

As soon as Jeffrey opened the door to his apartment, he heard a sneeze. When he went to his room, he saw a tissue float up. He heard a sniffle. Then a crumpled tissue flew into the wastepaper basket.

"This cold is terrible," Bradford said. "At dinner tonight, ask your mother to make me some hot cocoa."

When Jeffrey asked for hot cocoa, his mother asked him why he wanted something hot to drink in the middle of the summer.

"I just feel like having cocoa," Jeffrey said.

Achoo! Bradford sneezed.

Jeffrey's mother dropped the pan she was holding. "That's the loudest sneeze I've ever heard," Jeffrey's mother said as she handed him a tissue. "You'll have to stay in bed tomorrow."

"But I don't have a cold."

Jeffrey spent the next day in bed while Bradford sat in the desk chair and sneezed. Jeffrey's mother brought him a cup of hot

chicken soup. When she left the room, Bradford drank the soup.

The next morning Jeffrey asked Bradford to please try not to sneeze. Jeffrey didn't want his mother to tell him to stay in bed for another day. It was the day of the game against the Zebras.

While Jeffrey ate breakfast in the kitchen, Bradford stayed in the bedroom with a blanket over his head.

Bradford walked with Jeffrey to the park. Bradford sneezed a few times. A woman waiting for a bus told Jeffrey, "Go home and take care of your cold."

When Jeffrey and Bradford got to the park, most of the other players on the team were already sitting on the ground, in a circle around Mr. Evers. They were all very quiet. Jeffrey sat with them.

"You all seem rather nervous," Mr. Evers said with a smile. "You shouldn't be. This is just a game. Just do your best."

Mr. Evers read the lineup to his team. Then the game began.

The Ghosts were the first team to bat.

Laura sat next to Jeffrey and whispered, "Is he here?"

"Yes. He came with me."

"Tell Bradford we need his help. We just *have* to win this game."

"But I don't know where he is," Jeffrey said.

Then Mr. Evers called to Laura, "Come on, you're up."

Laura grabbed a bat. She walked to the plate, took a few practice swings, and waited. The first pitch was low. The next one was coming in waist-high, straight over the plate. Laura swung. She hit the ball along the ground. The boy playing shortstop fielded it. But he threw it high, over the first baseman's head. Laura ran to second base.

"Thanks, Bradford," Laura said.

Laura went to third base on a fly ball that was caught by the right fielder. The next batter singled and Laura scored.

In the second half of the inning, with two outs, one Zebra player walked. The next hit a single. Then a ball was hit along the ground between Jeffrey and Laura. Jeffrey ran far to

his right, caught the ball, and threw it to first. The batter was out. No runs were scored.

Some of the people sitting in the stands cheered as Jeffrey ran off the field. Mr. Evers and a few players on the team patted him on the back. "Nice play," they said.

"Bradford is out there," Laura told Jeffrey. "I think we're going to win."

Jeffrey batted in the second inning. He hit a high fly ball that the left fielder caught.

In the third inning the score was still Ghosts 1, Zebras 0. The Zebras hit two singles. The next batter struck out. There was another single. Then the pitcher walked the next two batters. Two runs scored.

Mr. Evers, Jeffrey, Laura, and Paul, the third baseman, gathered around the pitcher. Mr. Evers smiled. "Just relax," he told the pitcher.

The pitcher took his time with the next Zebra batter. The runners waited a few feet off first, second, and third base. Then, on the third pitch, the Zebra batter hit a hard, low line drive over third base. Paul dove for the ball. He caught it. The batter was out. Then Paul stepped on third base. The runner couldn't get back in time. He was out too. The inning was over.

It was a great play. Fans in the stands cheered. Mr. Evers hugged Paul. And Laura whispered to Jeffrey, "Bradford must have caught that ball and pushed it into Paul's glove."

No more runs scored until the last inning. The score was still Zebras 2, Ghosts 1, when Laura came to bat. She hit the ball over the third baseman's head for a single. The next batter struck out. Then Paul hit a fly ball over the first baseman's head for a double. Laura went to third base. The next batter hit a line drive to the shortstop. He caught the ball for the second out. Then Jeffrey was up. There were still runners on second and third base.

Jeffrey remembered what Bradford had told him. He didn't hold his bat too high. When the pitch came in, Jeffrey swung level and hit the ball hard. He didn't look to see where it went. He just ran.

Mr. Evers stopped Jeffrey at first base. The ball had gone along the ground between the first and second basemen for a single and Laura and Paul had scored. The Ghosts were ahead 3 to 2.

The next batter hit a high pop-up. The second baseman caught it for the third out. It was the Zebras' turn to bat.

Jeffrey stood near second base. He punched his fist into the pocket of his glove and waited. Three more outs and the game would be over.

Chapter

·9·

"Come on, Bradford," Jeffrey said. "We really need you now."

The first Zebra batter hit a fly ball over Jeffrey's head. The center fielder ran in and caught it.

"That's one out," Jeffrey said softly.

The next Zebra batter hit a line drive over Laura's head. Laura jumped but couldn't reach it. The left fielder ran in. He caught the ball on the first bounce. He threw it to Jeffrey, but the runner was already standing on second base.

On the first pitch the next Zebra hit a foul ball behind home plate. The catcher took two quick steps back and fell. The ball dropped right into his glove.

"Thank you, Bradford," Jeffrey said softly. "That's two outs."

The people in the stands were cheering

wildly. Some were calling for a strikeout, others were hoping for a hit. Mr. Evers was clapping his hands and walking in circles behind the team bench.

The Zebra batter swung and missed the first pitch. The next pitch was high for a ball. The batter swung and hit the third pitch high over Jeffrey's head. The runner on second base ran toward third. Jeffrey turned. The ball was over the center fielder's head too. He ran back with his glove held high over his head.

"He caught it!" Jeffrey shouted.

"You mean Bradford caught it," Laura said as she and Jeffrey ran toward the pitcher's mound.

Mr. Evers ran onto the field. The team and some fans crowded around him. They lifted him up and cheered. The Ghosts were the Summer League champions.

When the center fielder joined the crowd, his teammates shook his hand. They patted him on the back and told him that his catch won the game.

"They should be shaking Bradford's hand," Laura told Jeffrey.

The Zebra coach and a few of the Zebra players came over to Mr. Evers. They shook his hand. Then the umpire came over with a large cardboard box.

Mr. Evers told his team to sit on the ground. Then he opened the box. It was filled with gold trophies. Mr. Evers gave one to each of the Ghost players.

Jeffrey and Laura waited until everyone else had gone. Then they walked all over the field calling for Bradford. But he didn't answer.

"Maybe Bradford is angry," Laura said as she and Jeffrey walked home. "Maybe he thinks that he should have a trophy too."

"I don't think so," Jeffrey said. "I think he's upset. He always said that we should win on our own."

"Well, the Zebras shouldn't have told a nice man like Mr. Evers that he was too old to coach. I'm glad Bradford helped. And I'm glad we won."

As they walked, Laura held her trophy up over her head. At one corner she told a few people about the game. She told them that the Ghosts were a team of leftovers. "And the leftovers won," she said.

Jeffrey walked with Laura to her house. Then he walked home alone.

Jeffrey wondered about Bradford. *Maybe Bradford doesn't really live here. Maybe he came just to help us win the championship,* Jeffrey thought. He had heard stories about ghosts who helped people for a short while and then were gone.

Jeffrey opened the door of his apartment. It was quiet. Jeffrey already missed Bradford.

Kerchoo!

Jeffrey ran to his room. Around his bed was a pile of crumpled tissues.

Kerchoo!

A tissue floated up and then dropped onto the floor.

"Did you win?" Bradford asked.

"You know we won. You helped us."

"No, I didn't. I didn't even stay to watch the game.

"My cold was really bad. I kept sneezing. I came home and went straight to bed."

"That's great," Jeffrey said. "I don't mean it's great that you have a cold. I mean it's great that you weren't at the game. That means that we won it by ourselves. Then we really *are* champions."

Jeffrey danced around, with the trophy held high over his head. Then he said to Bradford, "Well, let me tell you about the game. The score was three to two. I got the winning hit."

Then Bradford sneezed. It was a loud, booming sneeze.

Jeffrey laughed and said, "I'm glad you weren't at the game. Your sneeze could frighten a ghost, maybe even a whole baseball team named the Ghosts. And if you sneezed when I was batting, maybe I wouldn't have made the winning hit!"